KU-674-945

but she has no one to share it with.

Lily has a bike

but no one to ride with.

Lily wears a tutu

but she has no one to dance with.

Lily throws her ball

but she has no one to chase it.

Lily puts on high-heeled boots,
a hat and a feather boa

but she has no one to dress up with.

"Let's ride down this hill,"
Lily says to the snail.

But the snail is too slow.

"Do you want to dance?"
Lily says to the mouse.

But the mouse runs away.

"Chase my ball,"
Lily says to the chicken.

But the chicken is too silly.

"Shall we dress up?"
Lily says to the goat.

But the goat
chews the hat.

Lily sighs. "I have no one to play with,"
she says and kicks her ball.

The pig brings it back.

Lily rides away on her bike.

The pig follows.

Lily puts on her high-heeled boots and her hat.

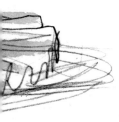

The pig cocks his ears at her.

Lily twirls on her toes.

The pig trots in a circle.

"Shall we go and get
a strawberry ice-cream?"
Lily says to the pig.

So they do,
and Lily and the pig
eat it all up.

To my good friend Emily Madeline MacLeod – J.A.H.
For Ruby and Harvey – J.B.

Little Hare Books
an imprint of
Hardie Grant Egmont
Ground Floor, Building 1
658 Church St
Richmond, Victoria 3121, Australia

www.littleharebooks.com

Text copyright © Janet A. Holmes 2011
Illustrations copyright © Jonathan Bentley 2011

First published 2011
First published in paperback 2012

All rights reserved. No part of this publication may be reproduced,
stored in a retrieval system or transmitted in any form or by any means,
electronic, mechanical, photocopying, recording or otherwise,
without the prior written permission of the publisher.

Cataloguing-in-Publication details are available from the
National Library of Australia

ISBN 978 1 921894 10 7

Designed by Vida & Luke Kelly
Produced by Pica Digital, Singapore
Printed through Phoenix Offset
Printed in Shen Zhen, Guangdong Province, China, June 2012

5 4 3 2 1